SPEAKING TO AN
ELEPHANT

AND OTHER TALES FROM
THE KADARS

RETOLD BY

Manish Chandi and Madhuri Ramesh
(based on oral stories narrated by the Kadars)

ILLUSTRATIONS: Matthew Frame

I

GOD'S FEAST

Kadavul, the creator, made all the people of this world: people from the hills, from the plains, and even those who went to live in towns. One day, he invited them all to his place for a great feast. He wanted to give them all special gifts, and a range of skills for living in this world.

People came from the hills, plains, and the city to join in the feast. As they arrived, they were shown into a huge building. It was a strange place with no walls, just enormous pillars crowned with a roof. The people Kadavul had created filled the space.

Each of them was given a seat, in front of a large leaf filled with food. After they had all eaten their fill, Kadavul announced that it was time for him to grant skills and gifts to each one. He asked them to step forward, one by one.

The people from the plains went up first, holding up the ends of their *veshtis* to receive their due. "Here are your gifts!" said Kadavul and poured seeds, stalks, roots and fruits into their veshtis.

Then Kadavul called the city folk. They unravelled their shawls and turbans – but they didn't get much, only a few shining pieces of metal. Nevertheless, they wrapped these strange objects into their turbans and shawls quickly, and carefully set them aside.

"NOW FOR YOUR SKILLS!" DECLARED KADAVUL. "YOU WILL ALL RECEIVE WHAT SUITS YOU BEST."

"To the people of the plains, I give the art of cultivation and of tending animals. Some of you in the towns will work with metals, others with money," announced Kadavul.

Meanwhile, the people from the hills waited and waited for Kadavul to call on them. Some of them had eaten a lot, grown tired of waiting, and wandered off. Others were half-asleep on the floor, reclining against the giant pillars.

So when Kadavul finally looked in their direction, they could barely get up. They just stretched out their hands from around the pillars. Nonetheless, Kadavul showered them with tools, seeds and tubers.

After receiving their gifts, they tried to pull back their hands but found them locked around the pillars. Eventually Kadavul's bounty slipped through their fingers and scattered around everywhere.

Looking down at what little gifts they had left in their hands, the hill people were very upset. They threw them away in disappointment. But an amazing thing happened. From the scattered gifts sprang a thick forest with a canopy of trees.

IT WAS FULL OF MARVELS: FLOWING RIVERS, HIDDEN ROCKS, FLITTING INSECTS, SCREECHING BIRDS, AND ALL KINDS OF CREATURES LARGE AND SMALL.

Kadavul was delighted and decided to bless the hill people. For after all, had they not helped create a beautiful forest? He said that they ought not to be disappointed anymore.

"Don't worry. You will live in the *kadu* or forest forever, and the forest will give you everything you need in order to live."

That is how the hill people came to be called the Kadars and only they can find the gifts of edible leaves, honey, tubers, soap-nuts, bamboo, turmeric and incense hidden in the forest.

2

HOW
THE KADARS AND
ELEPHANTS
BECAME FRIENDS

Sometime after Kadavul had given the Kadars their gifts, he decided to find out how they were faring. The forest they lived in had many wild and marvellous creatures, but not all of them were friendly to human beings.

Kadavul was particularly concerned about the large elephants that often lived right next to people. He wondered whom to ask. Then he remembered that some Kadars were expert story-tellers, and decided to ask one of them.

"Tell me," he said, "how do you live with the elephants? There are so many of them, and they are all very large."

"Oh, that's a long story. Let me tell you how we became friends with the elephants," said the story-teller and launched his tale.

"A long time ago, there was a brave young man in our village. He was a resourceful lad – he had accompanied his mother and father when they went deep into the forest to hunt and gather food, firewood and medicines.

ALL ALONG THE WAY, HE WOULD CAREFULLY OBSERVE MANY THINGS, AND STORE THEM AWAY IN HIS MIND.

When he was old enough to be independent, he decided to build himself a nice large *maadam*, a tree house, in the depths of the jungle. He chose a tall, broad tree and built his house between its spreading branches. The house would shelter him from sun and rain, and keep him safe from dangerous animals.

He was happy, exploring the forest, getting to know its smells, sights and sounds.

He and the wild creatures soon got used to each other and their different ways. All except the elephant.

One day, as he was sitting in his house, he saw an elephant limping past. She seemed in pain. When he looked closely, he noticed that a splinter had pierced her leg. He saw her stopping every now and then, trying to shake off the splinter but it remained stubbornly in place.

He looked about to see if the rest of the herd was nearby – he could see no sign of their presence. They must have moved ahead, he thought, leaving the lame elephant to find her way. Just as he was wondering what could be done, the elephant trumpeted in pain.

She was going round and round, and even as the young man watched her agony, she limped right to his door-step. She had come to seek shelter under his tree.

The young man made up his mind, and breaking off a sharp twig, came quietly down from his tree house.

He waited until the elephant turned her head away from him, and quickly, using his twig as a lever, he pulled the splinter out of her leg. But not a moment too soon, for the elephant turned around, startled, and twisted away. The young man stood his ground and held her eyes, and she stopped in her tracks...and slowly realized that her pain was in retreat. Then she turned away to find the rest of the herd.

THOUGH THE ELEPHANT WALKED AWAY, SHE DID NOT FORGET, AND ONE DAY, SHE WOULD RETURN.

One morning the young man was sitting in his tree house, looking around and thinking of a way to grow some crops when he saw an elephant approaching.

He stood up, startled, and backed away – because an elephant separated from her herd could be a dangerous creature. But then he realized that this elephant seemed to be looking for something. As she came closer, he realized that it was the elephant that had had a splinter in her leg.

When the elephant saw him, she waved her trunk and gently picked him up from his tree house and put him on her back. He was most surprised, but he also liked it.

The elephant then took him around the forest: at various places, she stopped to pull down fruits from trees, and dig tubers out of the soil… soon they had collected a huge pile of roots and fruits.

The young man was overwhelmed, and began to speak to the elephant, 'Thank you, but I can't eat all of this.' The elephant seemed to understand. 'I want to clear space in the jungle,' said the young man. 'I want to plant and harvest, fill my store with grain…'

No sooner had he said this than the elephant put him down and began to move away. He was surprised but sat down under a tree to wait.

He did not have to wait long. By and by, the elephant returned – with her herd! And before he knew what was happening they pulled down trees

and plants, trampling and shoving bushes and shrubs out of the way until a small part of the jungle was cleared. Then, trumpeting loudly, they began to move away…over to the next hill. Their work was done.

The young man stepped in to the cleared space and hurried to make a fence – he wanted to burn the shrubs and bushes, but did not want the fire to spread into the forest.

After the foliage was burned down, the fire subsided but the earth was still hot. He waited till the embers went cold, and then scattered some seeds over the ashes.

He knew that the rains would begin soon, and the seeds would sprout. 'May the harvest be bountiful' muttered the young man.

A few months later, just as the young man was getting ready to harvest his little field, he heard a familiar trumpeting sound. His elephant friends were back! He was delighted to see them, and decided that while he would harvest what he needed, he would leave behind stalks and some grain for the elephants.

This is the story of why and how our people can live alongside elephants – to this day.

WE SPEAK TO THE ELEPHANTS AND TELL THEM THAT WE TOO ARE OF THE FOREST AND THAT THEY NEED TO GO THEIR WAY JUST AS WE DO.

We do not trouble them and the elephants are grateful to us – all due to the good deed of that brave young man from long ago."

3

KADAVUL'S WEDDING

Each year, Kadavul celebrated his marriage. It was always at a particular time: during the season of rain, thunder and lightning. It was like no other wedding. For one, there was no bride or groom. It was just Kadavul, announcing to all his creatures that the time had come for earth and sky, rain and soil, to mix.

He then invited everyone to a big feast. All the animals in the forest were present to witness the grand spectacle, and they waited for it the whole year.

A week before the wedding, trees put out fresh leaves in preparation – bright green, soft pink and pale yellow. Green pigeons, black bulbuls and fairy bluebirds preened their feathers; vine snakes and pit vipers looked glossy in their new scales; and big cats, tigers and leopards, licked their paws and long furry tails clean. The entire forest was excited about the wedding. It was to take place on a big sheet of rock on top of the tallest hill in the Anamalai region.

On the big day, at dawn, the cicadas woke the entire forest up by chirping loudly. All the creatures set out immediately, hurrying to climb the large hill with the huge rock where the wedding was to take place.

ONLY AAMAI - A BIG BROWN TORTOISE THAT LIVED UNDER THE ROOTS OF A FIG TREE - LOOKED WORRIED. HE WAS WAS AFRAID THAT, ONCE AGAIN, HE WOULD BE TOO SLOW.

Each year he would set out to attend Kadavul's wedding – and every time, he would arrive almost five days late.

This year, at least, he wanted to make sure that he got there on time. For who knew how much longer he had to live?

"I am old and I have always been a slow walker. Can you help me get to the wedding on time?" he asked, looking up at Langur swinging on the branches of the fig tree.

"Hoo, hoo, hoo!" hooted Langur, and jumped away, laughing loudly.

Ongal the hornbill - who was sitting on a branch carefully arranging his feathers - heard Aamai pleading with Langur.

Ongal took pity on Aamai and said: "Alright, I'll take you. Just bite hard on my tail when I'm ready to take off and I'll carry you with me when I fly. But remember: NEVER look down or talk when I'm flying or you'll lose your grip and fall."

Aamai was overjoyed and agreed to follow Ongal's instructions carefully. Then Ongal got ready to fly, stretched his wings and held out his tail. Aamai clamped his mouth around it firmly. Ongal then flapped his large wings and they took off.

As they rose up in the air, all the animals in the forest looked up and chorused in amazement:

Ongalum naamaiyum barra-ro
thathaka pithaka chaadi kali
(Ongal and Aamai are speeding along with a jump here and a leap there)

The sound of their chanting reached Aamai, soaring above. He craned his neck to peer down.

THE ANIMALS DOWN BELOW ON EARTH LOOKED SO STRANGE AND SURPRISED...THEY WERE STARING OPEN-MOUTHED AT AAMAI FLYING. AAMAI FELT WONDERFUL.

31

"Ha! Ha!" he laughed, completely forgetting Ongal's instructions.

Aamai hurtled down to earth and broke the branches of a tall *surlimaram* as he fell. Ongal looked down and saw poor Aamai lying helplessly on the forest floor with his shell broken into thirty-six different pieces.

Ongal wanted to help his friend, but didn't know what to do. So he flew on – straight to Kadavul, to tell him the story of Aamai's plight.

As soon as the wedding was over, Kadavul went to the place where Aamai had fallen. With the help of the big black forest ants, Kadavul collected all the broken pieces of the shell and then joined them together carefully with tiny stitches.

Since Aamai had missed the wedding, Kadavul scattered some grains of rice that had been left over from the feast on the forest floor; those grains of rice changed into the delicate white kumin mushrooms that all tortoises like to eat.

And so it is that in the Kadar forest, even now, the kumin mushrooms last for just one day – the day of Kadavul's wedding. They never ever grow in the same place twice.

And if you look closely at a tortoise, you can still see those small stitch marks between the pieces of its shell.

4

THE GRASSHOPPER AND THE MOUSE DEER

The story of Aamai and Ongal is one that our people repeat with wonder, each time a tortoise crosses our path, or when we happen to chance on a kumin mushroom. We tell each other such stories to remind ourselves of Kadavul's ways, of why some things are the way they are.

The story of the grasshopper and the mouse deer is another favourite amongst us.

Deep in the forest, in a valley across which flowed a gurgling stream, there was a huge fallen tree. It was covered with velvety moss; insects and snails crawled all over it.

All the animals in the valley would come to drink cool water from this stream, and smaller creatures often rested for a while under a dense *kurinji* shrub a few metres away.

Vettukilli was a green grasshopper who lived on the lowest branch of the kurinji shrub, between the petals of its bright blue flowers. He was a talkative insect and often got into trouble because he talked too much.

One evening, he saw Kooran the mouse deer running about, jumping this way and that, across the stream and back again.

MOUSE DEER ARE SMALL AND VERY SHY ANIMALS, ONLY AS BIG AS LARGE HOUSE CATS, SO VETTUKILLI WAS NOT IN THE LEAST AFRAID OF HER.

When Kooran came close to the kurinji shrub, she stopped to catch her breath, and Vettukilli took the chance to begin chattering:

"Kooran! I haven't seen you in a long time. Where have you been all these days? Why are you running so fast?"

"I've been away at the other end of the valley, but I can't stop and chat with you now Vettukilli! Pitthakannu is after me! I've got to hide. I'm tired, I've been running for hours."

Then she peeped out to warn him: "You're a chatterbox, Vettukilli, but if Pitthakannu comes around and asks you where I am, please don't say a word. If she catches me, she'll swallow me whole!" Vettukilli closed his big glassy eyes, nodded, and promised to be quiet.

Sure enough, Pitthakannu appeared in a while, her paws moving silently but surely over rocks of the stream, sniffing around and searching for Kooran. She then spotted Vettukilli sitting on the lowest branch of the kurinji shrub, and growled: "Did you see Kooran run this way? Where did she go?"

Vettukilli was very excited: this was the first time he had met Pitthakannu at such close quarters. He opened his mouth to answer the big cat, when he suddenly remembered his promise to Kooran. So he shut up immediately, but he was so excited that he couldn't help hopping in the direction of the place where poor Kooran was hiding.

Wily Pitthakannu understood what Vettukilli's jumping around meant. She went straight to the fallen tree and sniffed all around it, trying to find Kooran.

But Kooran was in luck. A smelly civet had slept under the tree the previous night, so Pithakannu could not catch Kooran's scent. She prowled around for a long time growling and sniffing, but finally gave up and wandered away, grumbling.

Kooran jumped out of her hiding place. She was furious with Vettukilli for nearly giving away her hiding place. He needed to be taught a lesson! She decided to frighten the grasshopper, so that he would never ever give away a secret again.

"What made you jump like that, you stupid creature? You nearly had me in the jaws of Pitthakannu!" she shouted. "If you ever do that again, I'll come back and stamp you hard with my golden shoes!" She stamped her small sharp feet on the ground till the kurinji shrub shook to and fro, and Vettukilli almost fell off the lowest branch. Looking sharply at him one last time, Kooran darted away into the forest.

FROM THEN ON, VETTUKILLI LIVED IN FEAR OF KOORAN'S SHARP GOLDEN SHOES. HE STILL HOPPED HERE AND THERE, BUT HE WAS CAREFUL NOT TO POINT ANYWHERE.

And that's why, to this day, grasshoppers skip restlessly around – but never in any particular direction.

5

THE FOREST
IS OUR HOME

There are many stories and tales about jungle creatures that we tell each other. That is how we get to know their ways, after all we share a home with them.

One of these tales is the story of how the Kadars came to be forest-dwellers. It was Kadavul's wish that we always live in the forest – and the forest would give us everything we need to live. There is another story of how Kadavul taught us to eat, to take what we need and nothing more.

ONE DAY KADAVUL CAME TO VISIT THE FOREST AND CALLED ON THE KADARS TO SHOW HIM AROUND, AS THEY KNEW IT SO WELL.

Together, they roamed the length and breadth of the jungle through hills, grasslands, and thick forests. They walked through valleys where they could camp on sheet rock and drink water from the streams. They walked and climbed for most of the day, resting very little. Finally, by evening, the Kadars were tired and hungry. A few of them decided to stop and eat what they brought from home: a meal of millet and tubers.

The eldest Kadar was not sure. "Let's wait," he said. "Kadavul wants to see more of the forest. Look, he's already speeding ahead. He has something special in store for us."

"It's hard to keep pace with him. We're hungry!" grumbled some of the younger Kadars. They slipped behind some trees, and began to eat their food. The older ones shook their heads and huried to catch up with Kadavul. Finally, Kadavul stopped at a large rock on a tall hill.

He asked the Kadars to bring large leaves from the forest, and when everyone was seated before a leaf, he made the most delicious meal appear: there was grain, meat, greens and fruit of every description.

As they were beginning to eat, the younger Kadars - who had stayed behind to eat by themselves - came up the hill, looking downcast.

The older Kadars knew that the younger ones would not be able to eat, since they were already full.

When Kadavul heard this, he was very displeased. After all, he had created this feast for everyone, and now it appeared that some of them had eaten without inviting him to share their food.

In a fit of anger, Kadavul threw all the food away into the forest.

"You have eaten out of turn, without sharing your food with others. From now on you won't be able to eat as before. You have to look for food, search and gather, dig and store."

And that is why, to this day, we collect honey and soap-nuts, bamboo and tubers, greens and wild ginger… and everything else we need from the forest floor and the branches of trees.

BECAUSE WE WANDER THE FOREST, LOOKING FOR THINGS, WE KNOW WHAT GROWS WHEN AND FOR HOW LONG, WHAT IS TO BE EATEN, AND WHAT IS TO BE AVOIDED, WHAT PLANTS ARE USEFUL AS MEDICINE…

Because of the lesson Kadavul taught us, we are also very careful.

We think of how much we may take of this root, how much of that fruit… we take only what we need, because we have to share this forest with all creatures. It is our common home.

Even the young Kadars who want to go away and work in the plains these days agree with that.

AUTHORS' NOTE

The Kadars are an adivasi community who live in the Anamalai and Parambikulam hills, along the state borders of Tamil Nadu and Kerala in South India. They say that in olden times, the Kadars used to trade forest products like honey, beeswax, cardamom, roots and tubers with the plainspeople of Kongu Nadu.

In the 19th century when the British began to use the forested hill ranges of the region for tea plantations, the Kadars worked as their guides and coolies. Since they knew the region well, they showed the British safe paths around these dense forests and carried heavy materials across the steep hills. A few Kadars did try to work in the tea and coffee plantations that were being created but most preferred to depend on the forest for their needs.

Today, there are about 20 Kadar settlements, all within national parks and wildlife sanctuaries of the Anamalai and Parambikulam hills. They are one of the smallest groups of adivasi communities in India – their largest settlement has only about 250 people. After many years of change, more Kadars now work in the plantations and plains while still living close to or within their forest homes; but a few others still live off the forest. Several are expert guides who assist tourists and scientists in exploring these forests.

The Kadars call their language 'AAL ALAAPPU' and over the years they have added many words from Malayalam and Tamil too. Although they do not maintain written records, they are excellent story-tellers with many stories of animals, plants and people from the hills where they live. Elderly Kadars in particular tell these stories about the forest around them to their children and grandchildren, reminding them of their ancestors and how they lived in the forest.

It is from such friends, old and young, that we first heard the stories in this book: we are grateful to S. Ganesan, Vijaya and Padmini of Erumaparai; Thangaraj, Dinesh and Ganesan of Nedunkundru; Elsieammal of Kavarkal; Jayamani of Eethukuzhi and Shantammal of Udumanparai for generously sharing many stories and cups of *kattan chaya* with us.